CARTOON NETWORK™

MONKEY SEE, DOGGY DO

Adapted by Laura Dower from
the "Monkey See, Doggy Do" storyboards by Don Shank

Based on "THE POWERPUFF GIRLS," as
created by Craig McCracken

WORLDWIDE PUBLISHING™

SCHOLASTIC INC.

New York   Toronto   London   Auckland   Sydney
Mexico City   New Delhi   Hong Kong

No part of this publication may be reproduced in whole or in part, or stored in a retrieval system, or transmitted in any form or by any means, electronic, mechanical, photocopying, recording, or otherwise, without written permission of the publisher. For information regarding permission, write to Scholastic Inc., Attention: Permissions Department, 555 Broadway, New York, NY 10012.

ISBN 0-439-16013-8

Special thanks to Bill Lesniewski for cover and interior illustrations.

Cover designed by Peter Koblish
Interiors designed by Mary Hall

12 11 10 9 8 7 6 5   1 2 3 4 5/0

Printed in the U.S.A.
First Scholastic printing, October 2000

THE CITY OF TOWNSVILLE!

Shhhhhhhhhh! Oops. Sorry!

The city of Townsville . . .

A city that sleeps . . .

A tired town with an early, early bedtime . . .

No need for late nights here . . .

Gotta get that beauty sleep . . .

Here in Townsville, everything is as peaceful as can be. The city is serene and safe. Nighttime is the right time — for a snooze. . . .

Out in the suburbs, Townsville citizens are tucked away in their beds.

Is Professor Utonium up working late on that unified theory?

"SNORE!" the Professor snored.

No, even our hardworking Professor Utonium has slipped into sleep. . . .

Just look at The Powerpuff Girls. Blossom, Bubbles, and Buttercup
are far away in their own dreamy slumber.
  Awww. Buttercup's brawling — even in her dreams! *Go get 'em, Girl!*
Yes, everyone's resting up for a bright new day. . . .

But back in the city, someone is NOT asleep.

Somewhere inside Townsville's museum, someone sinister is sneaking around.

Look! He's headed toward the magnificent Anubis Dog Head exhibit....

Oh, no! He's snipping the trip wire!

Oh, no! He's stealing the Anubis Dog Head!

Oh, no! He's snatching the Anubial Jewels!

Who *is* this shadowy villain?

THE TOWNSVILLE TRIBUNE

STOLEN!

BEFORE

AFTER

Who's got the Jewels?

Earlier today, the city of Townsville was terrorized by a jewel-grabbing joker! Officials at the scene say that they are following a few leads thanks to the help of The Powerpuff Girls. Blah blah blah. No one reads this stupid paper anyway.

Can Blossom, Bubbles, and Buttercup Save the Day—Again?

MUTT NO MORE

Bow WOW! For the Poodle in You!

Blossom took charge of the crime scene. "Girls! SPREAD AND SEARCH FOR CLUES!" Bubbles hustled down the hallway and ripped up the rug! *Nothing!*

Blossom plowed into paintings with a Powerpuff P-O-W! *Nothing!*

Buttercup sped up the stairs, leaving no step unsmashed! *Nothing!*

The curator cried out, "Aaaaargh!" as he fainted away. His museum was a miserable mess — and still NO clues!

9

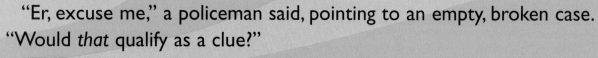

"Er, excuse me," a policeman said, pointing to an empty, broken case. "Would *that* qualify as a clue?"

"THE ANUBIAL JEWELS!" the Powerpuffs proclaimed.

The Anubial Jewels

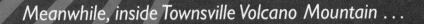

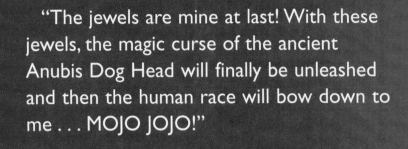

"The jewels are mine at last! With these jewels, the magic curse of the ancient Anubis Dog Head will finally be unleashed and then the human race will bow down to me . . . MOJO JOJO!"

Oh, no, Mojo Jojo! Say it ain't so so! Did he say *bow* down . . . or was that bow *wow* down? We sure hope those Powerpuffs are hot on his trail. . . .

11

"Gee, I sure wish we could find a trail," muttered Blossom. But then, she spotted something suspicious. "Look! That dog! He's trapped!"

The Powerpuffs zipped over.

"Poor puppy," said Bubbles.

"He must be one *hot* dog!" Buttercup blurted.

"Don't worry," Blossom called to the cornered canine. "We'll let you out!"

MALPH

MALPH'S MARKET

Woof! Rowf! Arf!

MALPH'S MARKET

"What's wrong, boy?" Blossom asked. "Who did this?"

The dog tried to tell the Girls. "Rowf, ruff . . . it was . . . rrrooof . . ."

"It was . . . *who*?" Blossom exclaimed. "Something funny is going on here."

Suddenly, the sound of barking filled the air. Dogs were everywhere — as far as the eye could see!

Buttercup pointed up in the sky. "The Powerpuff signal! Let's go!"

The three sisters sped away to the Mayor's office.

"What is it, Mayor?" Blossom demanded.

But then the Powerpuffs gasped. Townsville's Mayor had the body of — *a dog?*

"A sick plot is under way," the Mayor proclaimed. "And the madman responsible is . . . rrrruff . . ."

He looked to Miss Sara Bellum for help, but she wasn't quite herself today, either.

The Mayor tried to speak again. "The culprit in this caper is . . . Mmmo . . . Moh . . . Mmmmm . . . Mmrr . . . BOW! BOW-WOW WOW-WOW!"

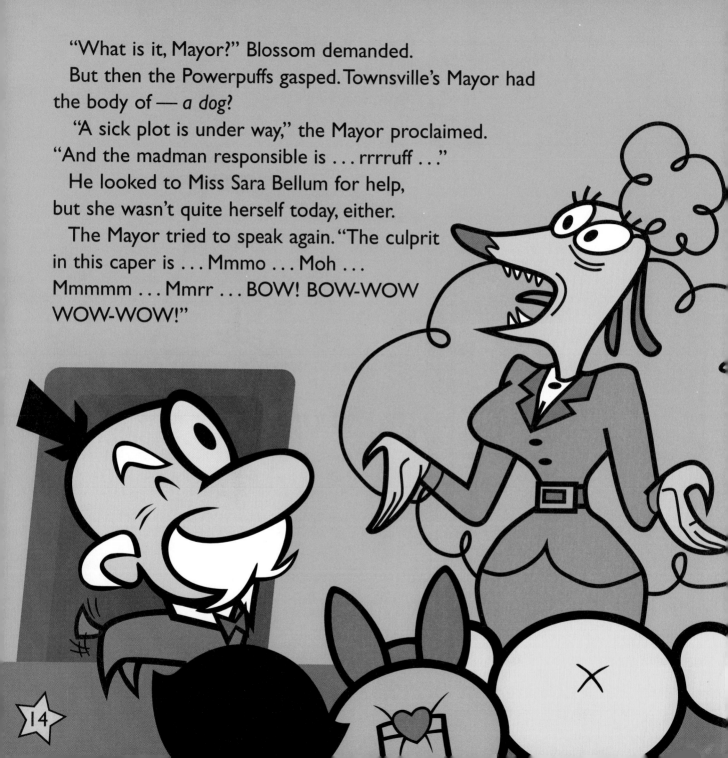

In the blink of an eye, the Mayor had turned one hundred percent pooch.

"Wheeee! Puppy!" Bubbles squealed.

"Okay, enough's enough, Bubbles," said Blossom. "We've gotta go see the Professor!"

"Puppy!" Bubbles giggled with glee, scratching the Mayor's tummy. Buttercup bellowed even louder, "Bubbles! C'mon! We've got work to do!"

Yes, it was a dog day afternoon in Townsville . . . *literally*! But how?

With the help of the evil Anubis Dog Head and the Anubial Jewels — that's how! Thanks to Mojo Jojo's heist, Townsville was *really* going to the dogs!

Drat that Mojo Jojo! How dare he turn man into man's best friend!

"All right, you miserable, flea-bitten curs! Heel!" Mojo shrieked.
The darting dogs stopped dead in their tracks — like zombies.
Mojo continued, louder (and meaner) than before. "I, Mojo Jojo, am your master, and you shall obey my commands like the dogs that you are. . . .

"Because I am your master, it is I who you will obey! And like the dogs you are . . . obeying commands is what you'll do!

"Now . . . SIT!"
The zombie dogs sat.
"Ha-ha-ha! Now . . . SPEAK!"
The zombie dogs howled.
"All right, all right, be quiet already! Now . . . STEAL!"
And with that, Mojo sent those mutts marching . . . to make
even more MAYHEM!

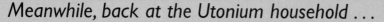

Meanwhile, back at the Utonium household . . .
"Professor!" Blossom called out, crashing through the front door.
"Bow-wow Wow-wow . . ." the Professor said, trotting over to the Girls.
Good heavens! The Powerpuff Girls couldn't believe their eyes! The Professor had gone pooch, too!

"Bow-wow Wow-wow," Professor Utonium declared in his deepest doggy baritone.

"Wait! I think he's trying to tell us something!" Blossom said.

The Powerpuffs pleaded, "C'mon, boy, what is it? Who's responsible for this, Professor? Tell us!"

Professor Utonium barked, "Bow-wow Wow-wow."

Bubbles blubbered, "Oh, noooo! It was *Bow-wow Wow-wow*?"

Blossom groaned, "No, Bubbles! I think he said *Mojo Jojo*!"

"Let's get that miserable monkey!" Buttercup cried.

The city was in chaos!
Mojo Jojo's mutts dodged into jewelry stores, gem palaces, and diamond shops — on a super stealing spree! To help with their getaway, they even stole a Cadillac from the car emporium!

Yes, it was crime time for these canines.
And no one was there to stop 'em!

Mojo was pleased, very pleased. His dogs were doing exactly as he had commanded.

"Ha-ha-ha-ha! Perfect! Now I have enough jewels for my master plan! My plan needs lots of jewels to make it work! Now I have enough of them! The jewels, that is . . ."

Mojo laughed like the maniac monkey he was.

DOGGED

Mojo needed all the jewels in Townsville to motor up his Anubial Transdogrifier.

He threw the jewels inside the Transdogrifier. He pulled down the switch. And then he turned an itty-bitty pink dial. . . .

"YESSS!" he screeched, watching the evil ray glow.

"I now have the power . . . for one gigantic . . . WORLDWIDE BLAST!"

Oh, no! Mojo was planning to put the whole planet into a doggy trance!

ON

POWER

"Now I, Mojo Jojo, will be true master of the world! When everyone in the world is a dog, its master will be me!"

And he cackled proudly to himself. . . .

Until some surprise visitors arrived in a blur of pink, green, and blue!

"Not so fast . . ." Blossom screeched.
". . . Mojo . . ." Buttercup screamed.
". . . Jojo!" Bubbles shrieked.
   But Mojo kept right on laughing.
"It's too late, Powerpuffs! Or
should I say . . ."

"PowerPUPS!"

Mojo zapped the sisters with his Anubial Transdogrifier. "You're no threat now, Powerpoochies. So why don't you be good doggies and let me get back to controlling the world. While you — STAY!"

But The Powerpuff Girls wouldn't give up so easily. Buttercup sniffed out the stolen Anubis Dog Head. It was sitting high on Mojo's machine. So the Girls, er . . . Pups . . . started to ram the machine. If the head were smashed, Mojo's sinister spell would cease!

Unfortunately, Mojo caught it just before it toppled to the ground.

"Lucky me!" Mojo shrieked. "If *this* had broken, the curse would have been broken! I am so lucky that it did not break!"

Now the sneering simian would make the Powerpups pay. . . .

Mojo sent his dastardly Dobermans after them!

But the Powerpups defeated Mojo's cruel canines! They turned and snarled at the mad monkey.

"Stay away, mangy mutts!" Mojo shouted, clutching the Anubis Dog Head.

While Mojo was busy ranting, Butterpup . . . er, Buttercup sneaked up behind him and . . .

CHOMP!

With one fierce bite, Mojo was toppled from his perch. The Anubis Dog Head went flying into the air — and crashed into a million pieces.

Crash! Smash! FLASH!

Suddenly, all over the world, one blinding light turned barks back into *words!* Dogs were people again! Townsville was a safe city once more!

The only dog around . . . was Mojo Jojo!

Bow-WOW! His Anubial Transdogrifier had reversed its spell . . . and turned that mad monkey into a miserable mutt.

Back home, The Powerpuff Girls reunited with the Professor and their brand-new family *pet*!

"Can we keep him, huh? Huh? Can we keep him, please? Can we, can we?"

"Now, Girls, it's a big responsibility keeping an evil villain in the house. You've got to feed him, water him, take him for walks, keep him from causing mayhem and from chewing the furniture. . . ."

So once again the day is saved, thanks to The Powerpuff Girls!